For Dan - S.S.

*Dedicated to my wife, Rayna. Without her support, I wouldn't
be able to draw silly, fun books about banana hunts - J.C.*

A TEMPLAR BOOK

First published in the UK in 2024 by Templar Books,
an imprint of Bonnier Books UK
4th Floor, Victoria House
Bloomsbury Square, London WC1B 4DA
Owned by Bonnier Books
Sveavägen 56, Stockholm, Sweden
www.bonnierbooks.co.uk

1 3 5 7 9 10 8 6 4 2

ISBN 978-1-80078-473-4

Edited by Amelia Warren
Designed by Chris Stanley
Production by Neil Randles

Printed in China

MIX
Paper | Supporting
responsible forestry
FSC® C104723
FSC
www.fsc.org

Banana Hunt

Suzy Senior   Josh Cleland

templar
books

"**OH NO,** that's too scary!" declared Auntie Dot.
"Let's find something else, something safer, to spot."

At last, something **PERFECT** popped into his head.

"Bananas!" he cried.

"We can hunt those instead."

He found a
HUGE
bunch,

then he staggered away
to hide them excitedly, all round the bay.

He put some in trees,

and one under a rock.

And one on a washing line, tucked in a sock.

Bernardo hid two in a log on the shore.

And three on a turtle...

and lots and lots and lots **more!**

Until the **whole bunch** had been hidden from view....

"**I'm finished!**" he called.
"Now it's all up to you!"

So, Auntie Dot hunted.

She lifted the rock.

She peeked in the log...

and she peered in the sock.

She went far and wide, and she looked high and low...

And collected so many bananas.

But OH...

... She started to wonder. "Bernardo," she cried. "How many of these did you **actually** hide?"

Bernardo looked puzzled.
"I'm really not sure...

I don't think I counted.
There might be **lots more!**"

"Don't worry," laughed Auntie.
"It's picnic time now."

"Oh, yes!" cheered Bernardo.
But suddenly… **"OW!"**

Banana!

Another was hidden just there!
He slipped on the skin and flew right through the air.

His Auntie rushed over. Except, with a...

SPLAT!

Banana!

Another one fell from her hat!

They finally opened their basket, but - **ooh!**

Banana! All squashed into mushy, brown goo!

Bernardo sat down on the blanket, then **Yuck!**

Banana! Now flat as a pancake... and stuck!

"I'm sorry it's such a disaster," he sighed.

"Bananas are something you JUST SHOULDN'T HIDE!"

Exhausted and sticky,
they slowly went back.

Except what was **THAT,** up ahead on the track?

But just then, guess what **tumbled** out of the trees...

And bounced off the bear, who fell down to her knees!

Bewildered and dazed,
with a small, grumpy **ROAR**,

the bear grabbed one
slowly, in one massive paw.

Banana!

She sniffed it, and bit
through the skin...

Then lumbered off home
with a big, happy grin!

"There **were** quite a few," said Bernardo. "Hooray!
I think my **bananas** have just saved the day!"

"Your hunt was fantastic!" declared Auntie Dot.
"Although," she admitted, "I hope that's the lot."

That evening, Bernardo was back home in bed.

When Dad popped his head through the branches and said:

"Sleep well, little darling!
I'm so glad you're back.

In case you get hungry, I've brought you. . ."

Banana Hunt

While you were reading this banana-tastic story, Bernardo hid **20** PINK BANANAS for you to spot!

Can you find them all?